The Birthday Car

DEAR CAREGIVER,

The *Beginning-to-Read* series is a carefully written collection of classic readers you may remember from your own childhood. Each book features text comprised of common sight words to provide your child ample practice reading the words that appear most frequently in written text. The many additional details in the pictures enhance the story and offer the opportunity for you to help your child expand oral language and develop comprehension.

Begin by reading the story to your child, followed by letting him or her read familiar words and soon your child will be able to read the story independently. At each step of the way, be sure to praise your reader's efforts to build his or her confidence as an independent reader. Discuss the pictures and encourage your child to make connections between the story and his or her own life. At the end of the story, you will find reading activities and a word list that will help your child practice and strengthen beginning reading skills.

Above all, the most important part of the reading experience is to have fun and enjoy it!

Shannon Cannon

Shannon Cannon,
Literacy Consultant

Norwood House Press • P.O. Box 316598 • Chicago, Illinois 60631
For more information about Norwood House Press please visit our website at *www.norwoodhousepress.com* or call 866-565-2900.

LIBRARY OF CONGRESS CATALOGING-IN-PUBLICATION DATA

Hillert, Margaret.
  The birthday car / by Margaret Hillert; illustrated by Kelly Oechsli.
  — Rev. and expanded library ed.
    p. cm. — (A beginning-to-read book)
  Summary: A young boy and his friends play with his birthday gift
—a new red car.
  ISBN-13: 978-1-59953-043-7 (library binding : alk. paper)
  ISBN-10: 1-59953-043-0 (library binding : alk. paper)
  [1. Cars—Fiction. 2. Toys—Fiction. 3. Birthdays—Fiction.]
  I. Oechsli, Kelly, ill. II. Title. III. Series: Hillert, Margaret.
Beginning to read series. Easy stories.
  PZ7.H558Bi 2007
  [E]—dc22   2006007888

Beginning-to-Read series (c) 2007 by Margaret Hillert.
Library edition published by permission of Pearson Education, Inc. in
arrangement with Norwood House Press, Inc. All rights reserved.
This book was originally published by Follett Publishing Company in 1966.

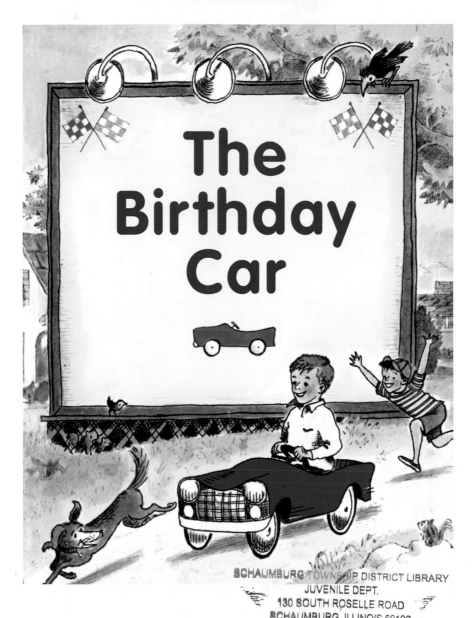

The Birthday Car

by Margaret Hillert
Illustrated by Kelly Oechsli

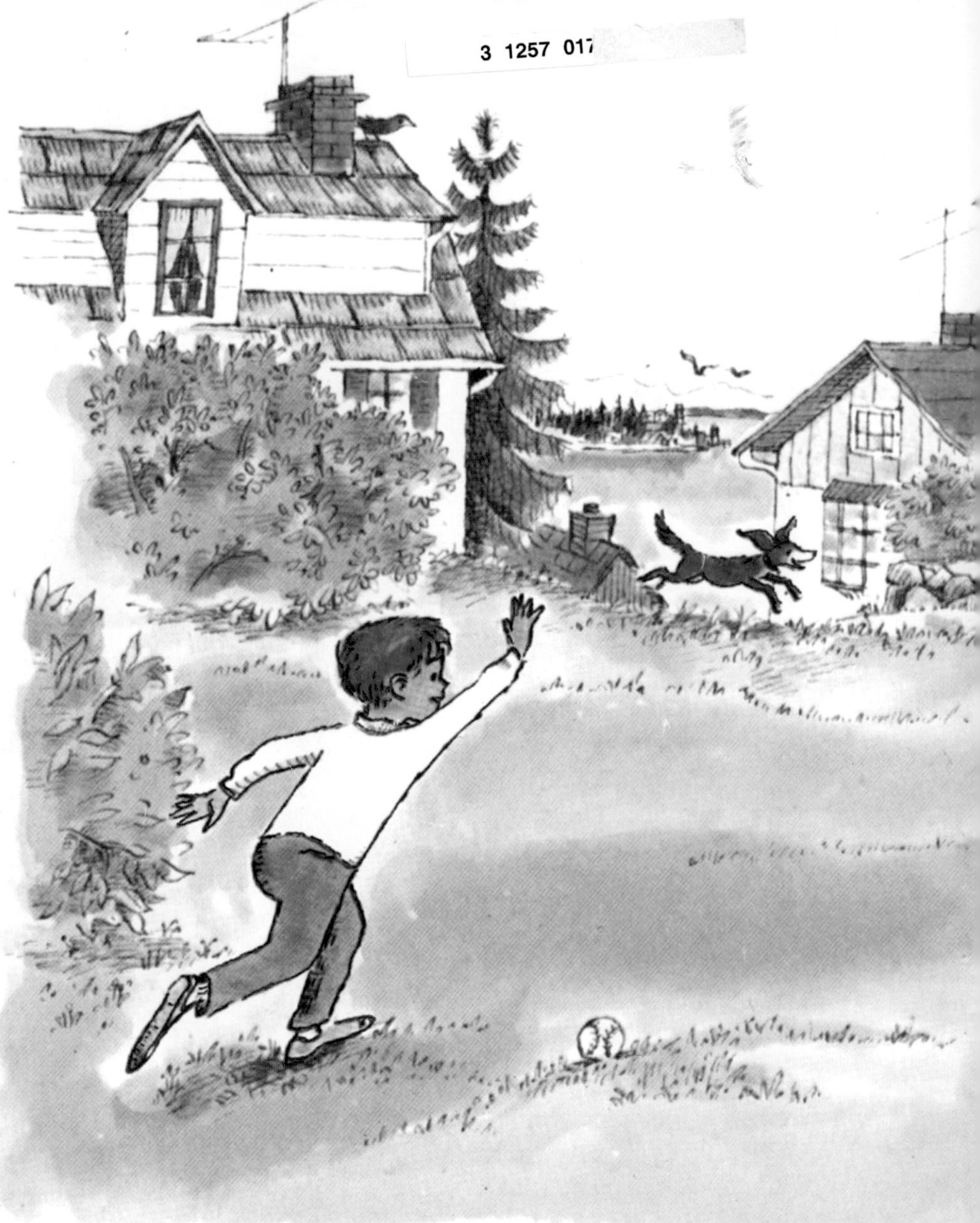

Father said, "Come here.
Come here.
Run, run, run.
Come and find something."

Father said, "Look, look.
Hero is something for you."

Oh, oh, oh.
A little red car.

I can go.
I can go away.
Away, away, away.

Oh, my.
Oh, my.
See me.
It is fun.

I can go up.
Up, up, up.

I can come down.
Down, down, down.

Here is a little blue car.
Come and play.

Here is a little yellow car.
Come and play.
Come and play.

One, two, three cars.
Three little cars.
Red, yellow, and blue.

Three little cars can go.
Away, away, away.
Away we go.

Oh, look.
Here is something.
Something big.
Come and play.

Look here, look here.
Here is something little.
It can go.
Come and play.

See something.
Come and play.

Here we go.

We can go up.

We can go down.

We can go to my house.

Father, Father.
Here we come.

Father said, "Come in.
Come in."

Oh, oh, oh.
A little red car is fun.

The following activities support the findings of the National Reading Panel that determined the most effective components for reading instruction are: Phonemic Awareness, Phonics, Vocabulary, Fluency, and Text Comprehension.

Phonemic Awareness: The /b/ sound

Sound Substitution: Say the words on the left to your child. Ask your child to repeat the word, changing the first sound to /**b**/:

kite = bite	felt = belt	pat = bat	fun = bun
corn = born	fox = box	leak = beak	path = bath
goat = boat	turn = burn	mall = ball	glue = blue

Phonics: The Letter Bb

1. Demonstrate how to form the letters **B** and **b** for your child.

2. Have your child practice writing **B** and **b** at least three times each.

3. Ask your child to point to the words in the book that start with the letter **b**.

4. Write down the following words and ask your child to circle the letter **b** in each word:

bat	cab	barn	rub	cub
bird	bib	bed	baby	book
marble	bit	tub	crib	maybe

Vocabulary: Compound Words

1. Explain to your child that sometimes two words can be put together to make a new word. These are called compound words. The story has two compound words: birthday, and something.

2. Write down the following words on separate pieces of paper:

news	plane	board	base	bed	fly
box	butter	week	ball	paper	room
sand	air	house	skate	dog	end

3. Help your child move the pieces of paper around to form compound words.
Possible answers: newspaper, airplane, skateboard, baseball, bedroom, butterfly, sandbox, weekend, doghouse

Fluency: Shared Reading

1. Reread the story to your child at least two more times while your child tracks the print by running a finger under the words as they are read. Ask your child to read the words he or she knows with you.

2. Reread the story taking turns, alternating readers between sentences or pages.

Text Comprehension: Discussion Time

1. Ask your child to retell the sequence of events in the story.

2. To check comprehension, ask your child the following questions:
   - Why do you think the title of the story is called *The Birthday Car*?
   - How many little cars were there in the book?
   - What other riding toys with wheels were there in the story?
   - Why did the children ride to the boy's house?
   - Do you think the boy in the story is friendly? Why or why not?
   - How do you celebrate your birthday?

WORD LIST

The Birthday Car uses the 39 words listed below.
This list can be used to practice reading the words that appear in the text.
You may wish to write the words on index cards and use them to help your
child build automatic word recognition. Regular practice with these words
will enhance your child's fluency in reading connected text.

a	down	I	oh	three
and		in	one	to
away	father	is	play	two
	find	it		
big	for		red	up
blue	fun	little	run	
		look		we
can	go		said	
car		me	see	yellow
come	here	my	something	you
	house			

ABOUT THE AUTHOR Margaret Hillert has written over 80 books for children who are just learning to read. Her books have been translated into many different languages and over a million children throughout the world have read her books. She first started writing poetry as a child and has continued to write for children and adults throughout her life. A first grade teacher for 34 years, Margaret is now retired from teaching and lives in Michigan where she likes to write, take walks in the morning, and care for her three cats.

Photograph by Glenna Washburn

ABOUT THE ADVISER Shannon Cannon contributed the activities pages that appear in this book. Shannon serves as a literacy consultant and provides staff development to help improve reading instruction. She is a frequent presenter at educational conferences and workshops. Prior to this she worked as an elementary school teacher and as president of a curriculum publishing company.